WHO SAID BOO?

WHO SAID BOO?

HALLOWEEN POEMS FOR THE VERY YOUNG

Written by **Nancy White Carlstrom**
Illustrated by **R. W. Alley**

Aladdin Paperbacks

For the wonderful students, teachers,
and staff of Woodriver Elementary School.

N. W. C.

To Cassandra, our Tinker Bell,
and Max, our Cowboy.

R. W. A.

First Aladdin Paperbacks edition September 1999

Text copyright © 1995 by Nancy White Carlstrom
Illustrations copyright © 1995 by R. W. Alley

Aladdin Paperbacks
An imprint of Simon & Schuster
Children's Publishing Division
1230 Avenue of the Americas
New York, NY 10020

Also available in a Simon & Schuster Books for Young Readers hardcover edition.
Designed by Carolyn Boschi
The text for this book was set in 14.5 point Lydian Bold
The illustrations were rendered in pen and ink and watercolor
Printed and bound in Hong Kong
10 9 8 7 6 5 4 3 2 1

The Library of Congress has cataloged the hardcover edition as follows:
Carlstrom, Nancy White.
Who said boo? : Halloween poems for the very young / written by Nancy White Carlstrom ; illustrated by R. W. Alley.-1st ed.
p.   cm.
ISBN 0-689-80380-7 (hc.)
Summary: A collection of poems celebrating such Halloween phenomena as monsters, witches, haunted houses, and jack-o'-lanterns.
1. Halloween-Juvenile poetry. 2. Children's poetry, American.
[1. Halloween-Poetry. 2. American poetry.]
I. Alley, R. W. (Robert W.), ill. II. Title.
PS3553.A7355W48 1995 811'.54-dc20 94-33577
ISBN 0-689-83151-X (pbk.)

The Poems

ON HALLOWEEN
NIGHT

This is the way the cat walks
Pit pat, pit pat
This is the way the cat walks
On Halloween night.

This is the way the moon walks
Tip tap, tip tap
This is the way the moon walks
On Halloween night.

This is the way the kids walk
Trip trap, trip trap
This is the way the kids walk
On Halloween night.

This is the way the wind walks
Rip rap, rip rap
This is the way the wind walks
On Halloween night.

This is the way the tree walks
*Scritch scratch,
scritch scratch*
This is the way the tree walks
On Halloween night.

*Pit pat
Tip tap
Trip trap
Rip rap
Scritch scratch*

BOO!

WHO SAID BOO?

BOO!

Did Mama say Boo?
No, Mama said Shoe.

Did Papa say Boo?
No, Papa said Who.

Did Baby say Boo?
No, Baby said Coo.

Did Sister say Boo?
No, Sister said Goo.

Did Brother say Boo?
No, Brother said Chew.

Did Grandpa say Boo?
No, Grandpa said Moo.

Did Granny say Boo?

Where's Granny?

Granny
said
Boo!

O000...

Granny who?

I'M A MONSTER!

I'm a monster
Be careful

I'm a monster
I can scare you

I'm a monster
If you let me

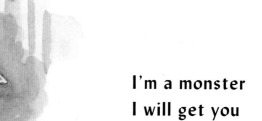

I'm a monster
I will get you

10

I'm a monster
In the mirror

Eeek!

I don't like what I see
Is that really me?

I'm a monster!

But please
Let me carry my mask!

MIXED-UP MASQUERADE

Rabbit's nose
Wiggle wiggle
Rabbit's tail
Puffball
Rabbit's paws
Soft fur
Rabbit's ears
Oh no!
Where did they go?

Where are Rabbit's ears?

Pig's tail
Curlicue
Pig's ears
Pink pink
Pig's feet
Plink plink
Pig's nose
Oh no!
Where did it go?

Where is Pig's nose?

Pelican's voice
Squawk squawk
Pelican's feet
Clap clap
Pelican's wings
Flap flap
Pelican's beak
Oh no!
Where did it go?

Where is Pelican's beak?

Owl's eyes
Wide-open
Owl's beak
Yellow sharp
Owl's ears
Tiny tufts
Owl's feathers
Oh no!
Where did they go?

Where are Owl's feathers?

Bear's stomach
Berry full
Bear's nose
Sniff snuff
Bear's growl
Grrr-rruf
Bear's paws
Oh no!
Where did they go?

Where are Bear's paws?

Mouse's tail
Teeny-tiny
Mouse's ears
Point up
Mouse's feet
Scriff scruff
Mouse's squeak
Oh no!
Where did it go?

Where is Mouse's squeak?

Rabbit ears
Pig nose
Pelican beak
Owl feathers
Bear paws
Mouse squeak
Somebody's sister
In a mixed-up masquerade

HAUNTED HOUSE

The haunted house
ooo-ooo
Is dark inside
ooo-ooo
Cat eyes glow
ooo-ooo
Bat wings glide
ooo-ooo
Are you afraid?
ooo-ooo

Please come with me
ooo-ooo

I'll take your hand
ooo-ooo
And we can be
ooo-ooo

BOO!
BOO!
BOO!

EEEEEK .!

Scared together!

HALLOWEEN CARNIVAL

I left my wig at the penny toss
My cape is hanging near the door
My gloves are floating in the tub
I'm not a vampire anymore.

I'm Me at the Halloween Carnival!

HOW MANY WITCHES?

How many witches on a broomstick?
How many black cats creeping by?
How many pumpkins in the garden?
How many full moons in the sky?

4–3–2–1
1–2–3–4

Knock!   Knock!   Knock!   Knock!
Open up the door!

WHO-O-O ARE YOU?

Click!   Clack!
Click!   Clack!
Who's that walking?

Plip!   Plop!
Plip!   Plop!
Who's that hopping?

Thump!   Bump!
Thump!   Bump!
Who's that jumping?

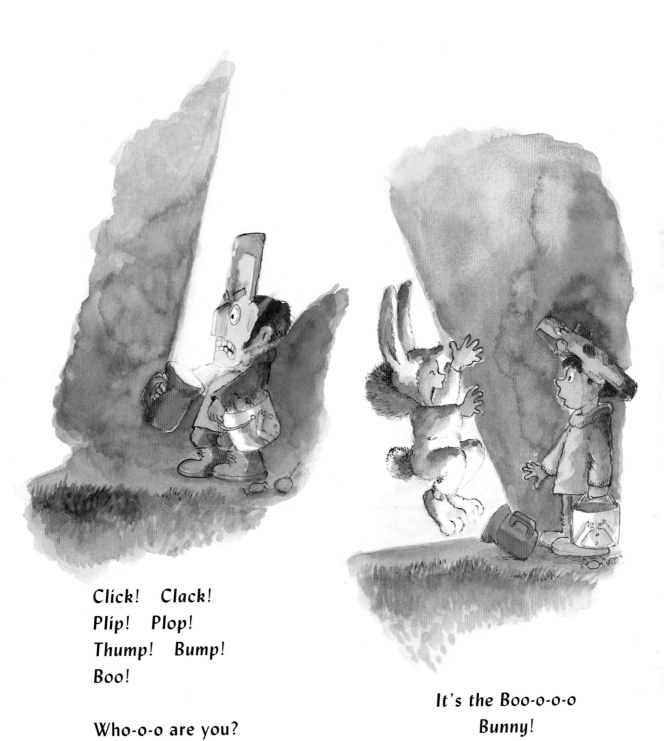

Click! Clack!
Plip! Plop!
Thump! Bump!
Boo!

Who-o-o are you?

It's the Boo-o-o-o
Bunny!

SOMEBODY'S TAPPING AT MY WINDOW

Somebody's tapping at my window
Somebody's knocking at the door
Somebody's creaking up the stairs

Somebody's brother snores!

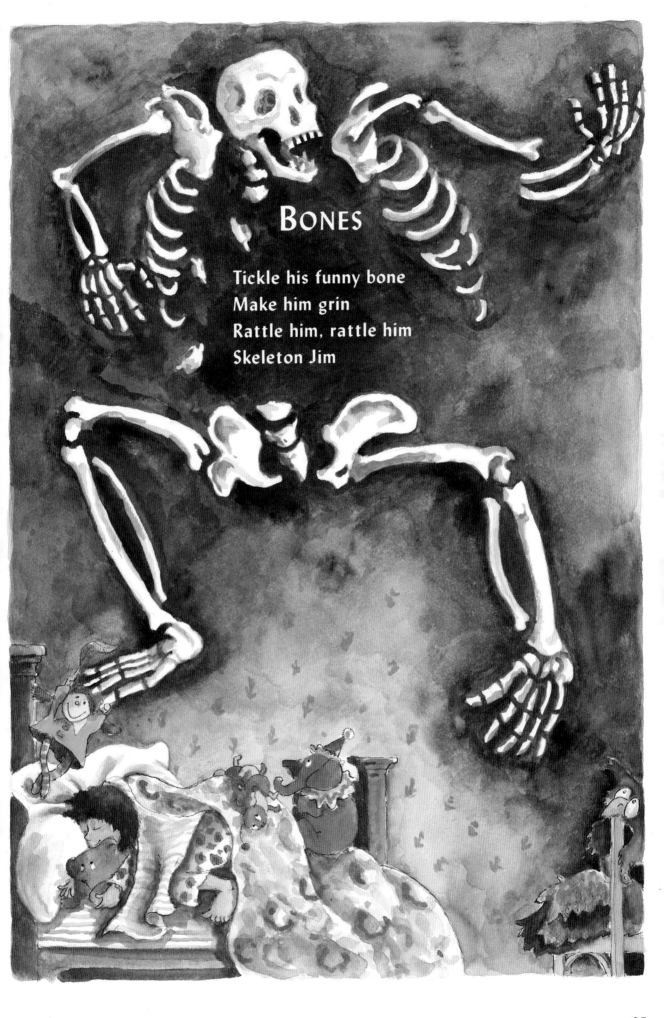

BONES

Tickle his funny bone
Make him grin
Rattle him, rattle him
Skeleton Jim

WHO'S AFRAID OF THE
BIG BAD SHADOW?

Who's afraid of the big bad shadow?
Swinging on the wall
Who's afraid of the big bad footsteps?
Running down the hall
Who's afraid of the scratching noise?
As the wind begins to call

I am! I am!
Mommy! Mommy!

Oh, Daddy was the shadow
Swinging on the wall
Daddy made the footsteps
Running down the hall
Daddy made the noise
As the wind began to call

Daddy's fixing the furnace
On Halloween night.

JACK-O'-LANTERNS

Get the pumpkins
Carve a grin
Lift the lid
Put a candle in.

Turn the lights out
Watch them glow
Jack-o'-lanterns
Seem to know

Just what to say
On Halloween night!

Trick or treat!
Good night!